P9-CLC-559

The Brave Little Parrot

STORY BY RAFE MARTIN

ILLUSTRATIONS BY SUSAN GABER

G. P. PUTNAM'S SONS

Once a little parrot lived in a green forest.

One day dark clouds gathered. Lightning flashed, thunder crashed, and a dead tree, struck by lightning, burst into flames. The wind began to blow, and soon bright sparks were leaping from tree to tree.

"Fire!" called the little parrot, smelling the smoke. "Fire! Run! Run to the river!" Then, flapping her wings, she flew swiftly toward the safety of the river's shore. After all, she was a bird and could fly away.

But as she flew, she saw below her many of the forest's great trees wreathed in flames. She saw that many animals were trapped by the fire, with no way to escape. Suddenly a desperate idea, a way to save them, came to her.

Darting to the river, she called to the animals already gathered safely there: "Elephants, please fill your trunks with water to spray on the flames! The rest of us can dip our bodies in the river. We can carry water in cupped leaves, too. Let's work together to save the forest and our friends!"

But the animals huddling on the shore moaned: "There's nothing anyone can do now, little parrot. It's too late."

"It's true," coughed the cheetah. "Fast as I am, the flames are faster."

"And powerful as we are," trumpeted the elephants, "we can't charge through flames."

"It's hopeless," the animals agreed.

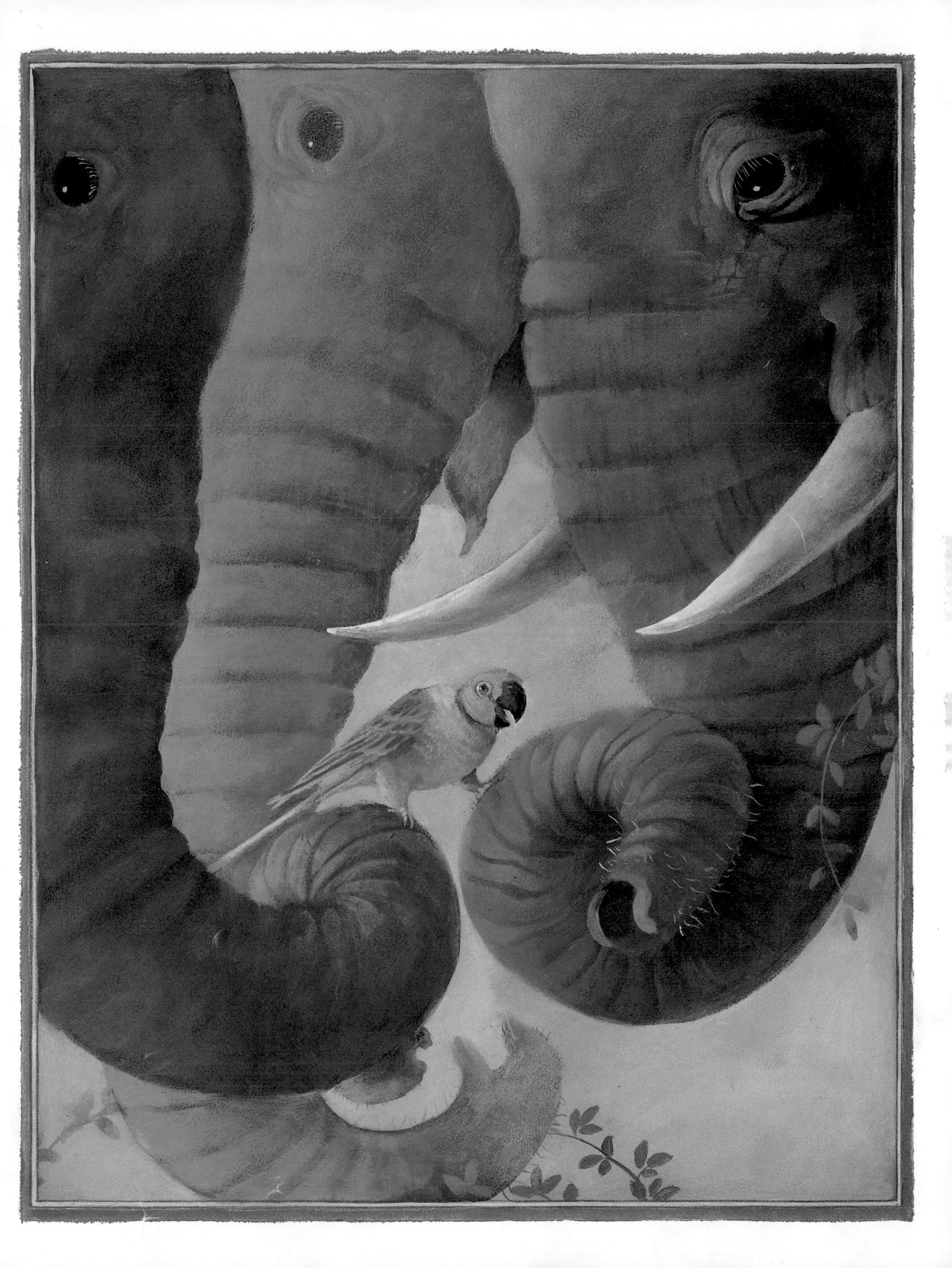

But the little parrot saw a way. After soaking her feathers in the cool water and filling a cupped leaf, she flew back over the burning forest.

Flames leaped at her. Fierce heat struck and thick smoke coiled. Walls of fire shot up now on one side, now on the other. But twisting and turning through the mad maze of fire, the little parrot flew bravely on.

At last over the heart of the burning forest, the little parrot shook her wings. The few drops of water that still clung to her feathers tumbled like jewels down into the flames. She poured the water from her leaf cup. The drops vanished instantly, with a *hssssssssssss!*

Then the little parrot flew back to the river. Once more she dipped her body and wings in the cool water and filled another leaf cup.

"Stay with us, little parrot!" pleaded the gentle deer. "Don't go back into the fire!"

"Yes! Stay!" roared the mighty tiger. "A few drops of water can't save a burning forest!"

"It's too late!" cried all the animals. "Be safe here with us!"

"But it might just be possible," panted the little parrot. "So I'll try." And once again she flew over the burning forest, shook her wings, and let those few glittering drops of water fall. *Hsssssssssssssss!*

Back and forth the little parrot flew, from the river to the forest, from the forest to the river. Her eyes burned red as coals. Her feathers were charred. Her claws cracked. She coughed and choked. But still the little parrot flew on.

Now at this time, some carefree goddesses and gods happened to drift by high overhead. They were laughing and talking in their palace of sunlit clouds. They were eating honeyed foods and sipping sweet wines. One of the gods happened to notice the little parrot flying far below. "Look!" he called. "Just look at that foolish bird trying to put out a forest fire with a few sprinkles of water!"

"Ridiculous!" snorted one.

"Impossible!" laughed another.

"Can't she see it won't work!" exclaimed the first god.

And putting down his golden bowl and silver cup, the god took on the shape of a golden eagle. Flapping his broad wings once, twice, three times, he dove down down down toward the little parrot.

As the little parrot again flew toward the forest's fiery heart, the eagle appeared by her side. "Go back, little bird!" he said in a majestic voice. "A few drops of water can't save a forest! Stop now and save yourself—before it is too late."

But the little parrot didn't turn back. "Great Eagle," she coughed, "time is running out. So I don't need advice. I just need help!" And on she flew.

The great eagle was amazed, for each instant the heat grew fiercer. He flapped his wings and rose up up into the cooler air high above.

Far below him now he saw the little parrot flying bravely on. Just above him the other gods and goddesses were laughing and talking, eating and drinking as the forest burned. Then, for the first time in all his endless life, that god felt ashamed. "We are gods, after all!" he exclaimed. "We should do something!"

And all at once the great eagle began to weep. Tears fell from his eyes, fell in torrents, sheet after sheet, like cooling rain, upon the fire, upon the forest, upon the animals, and upon the little parrot.

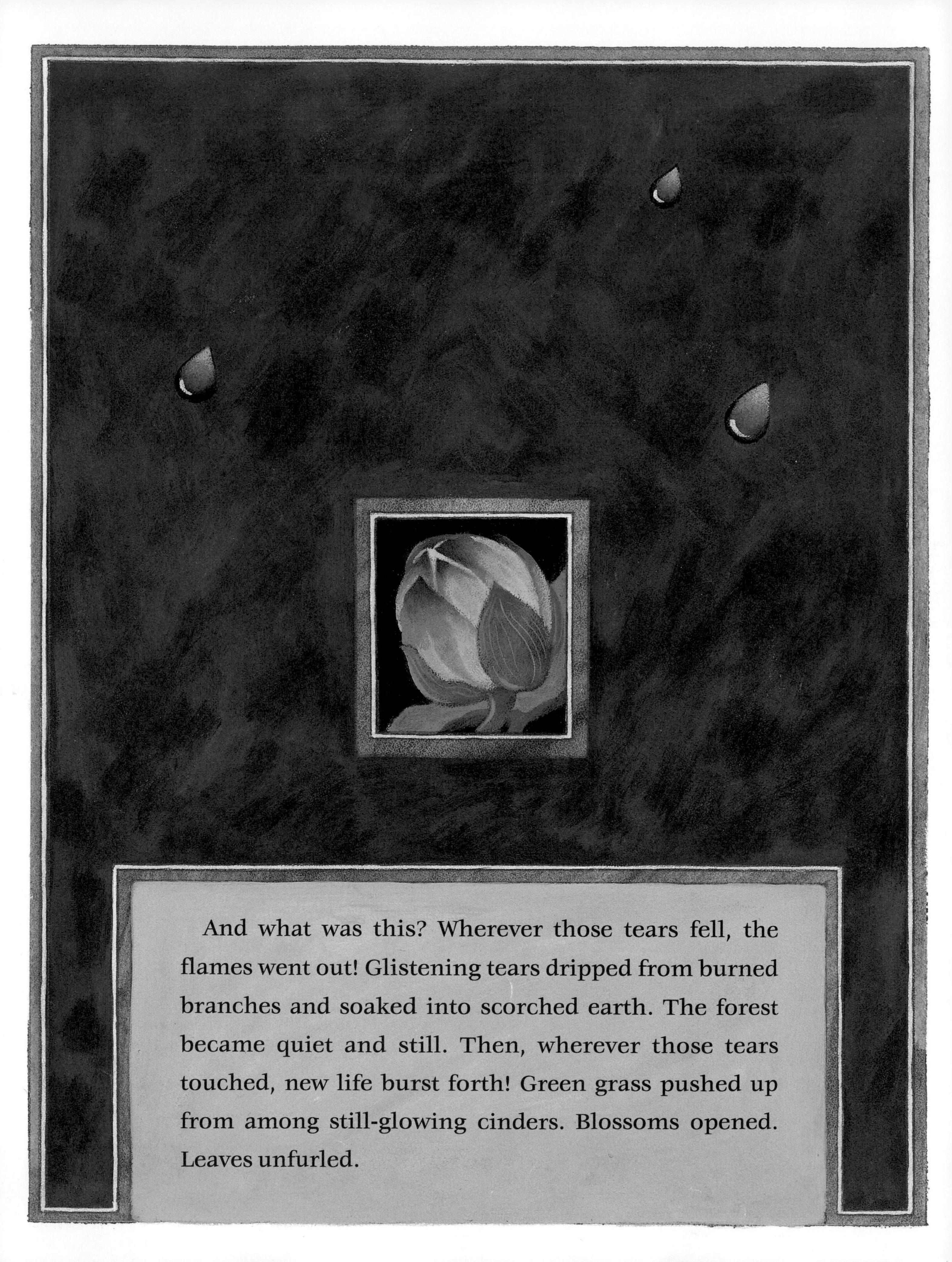

And what was this? Wherever those tears fell, the flames went out! Glistening tears dripped from burned branches and soaked into scorched earth. The forest became quiet and still. Then, wherever those tears touched, new life burst forth! Green grass pushed up from among still-glowing cinders. Blossoms opened. Leaves unfurled.

New feathers now grew on the little parrot, too—feathers red as flame, green as leaves, yellow as sunlight, and blue as a river! Such perfect colors! Such a pretty bird!

"The fire is out!" called the little parrot in her joy. "Look! The danger is past!"

The animals looked at one another in amazement. Washed by those tears, they were whole and well. Not one was harmed.

"Hurray!" cried the animals. "Hurray for the brave little parrot—and the miraculous rain!"

Overhead, in the clear blue sky, their friend the little parrot was looping and soaring in delight. She had done all she could, and somehow it had saved them.

What bird has done yesterday man may do next year.

—James Joyce, *Finnegans Wake*

For my teachers—R. M.

To Mom, Dad and Bruce—S. G.

A NOTE ON THE STORY

The Brave Little Parrot is a retelling of a traditional *jataka* tale from India, one of the stories about Buddha's past lives. Such stories are immensely popular throughout Asia and have been told and retold—and painted, carved, and dramatized—for 2,500 years. In our time, the tale of the brave little parrot brings precious drops of water to our imaginations. "Do the little thing that comes from *your* heart," it says, "and everything might change, in ways no one could imagine."

G. P. Putnam's Sons, a division of The Putnam & Grosset Group, 200 Madison Avenue, New York, NY 10016
G. P. Putnam's Sons, Reg. U.S. Pat. & Tm. Off. Published simultaneously in Canada.
Printed in Hong Kong by South China Printing Co (1988) Ltd. Design by Gunta Alexander. Text set in Veljovic
Library of Congress Cataloging-in-Publication Data
Martin, Rafe. The brave little parrot/story by Rafe Martin; illustrated by Susan Gaber. p. cm.
Summary: Because the brave little parrot does the thing that comes from its heart as it takes precious drops of water to the burning forest, things change in ways no one could imagine. [1. Jataka stories.]
I. Gaber, Susan, ill. II. Title. BQ1462.EM357 1998 294.3'823—dc20 95-14194 CIP AC ISBN 0-399-22825-X
1 3 5 7 9 10 8 6 4 2
First Impression